JUST GRANDMA AND ME

BY MERCER MAYER

A Random House PICTUREBACK® Book

Random House 🏠 New York

Just Grandma and Me book, characters, text, and images © 1983 Mercer Mayer. LITTLE CRITTER, MERCER MAYER'S LITTLE CRITTER, and MERCER MAYER'S LITTLE CRITTER and Logo are registered trademarks of Orchard House Licensing Company. All rights reserved. Published in the United States by Random House Children's Books, a division of Random House, Inc., New York. Originally published in slightly different form in 1983 by Western Publishing Company, Inc. PICTUREBACK, RANDOM HOUSE, and the Random House colophon are registered trademarks of Random House, Inc.
www.randomhouse.com/kids
Educators and librarians, for a variety of teaching tools, visit us at
www.randomhouse.com/teachers
Library of Congress Control Number: 82082653
ISBN-10: 0-307-11893-2   ISBN-13: 978-0-307-11893-6
Printed in the United States of America
22 21 20
First Random House Edition 2006

We went to the beach,
just Grandma and me.

I wanted to set up the beach umbrella,

but the wind was too strong.

I bought hot dogs for Grandma and me,
but they fell in the sand.
So I washed them off.

I found a nice seashell for Grandma, but it was full of a crab.

I wanted to blow up my sea horse,
but I didn't have enough air.
So Grandma helped a little.

I told Grandma to take me way out in the deep water,

but not too far.

I put on my fins and my mask
and showed Grandma how I can snorkel.

I dug a hole in the sand for Grandma.
Then I covered her up and tickled her toes.

I built a sandcastle just for Grandma, but a big wave came.

Grandma said that's what happens
to sandcastles, and we will build
a new one next time.

On the way home Grandma was tired,
so I told her I would watch for our stop.

We had a good time at the beach,
just Grandma and me.